The CABIN KEY

The CABIN KEY

BY Gloria Rand

ILLUSTRATED BY Ted Rand

Harcourt Brace & Company

San Diego   New York   London

Printed in Singapore

There it is—there's our mountain cabin, my favorite place in the whole world. While Mom and Dad start to unload the car, I get to unlock the cabin door. Dad just gave me the key.

Our family has come to this log cabin for years and years. First my great-grandparents, then my grandparents, then Mom and Dad, and now me.

Even if I shut my eyes, I know I'm at the cabin. It smells so good, so woodsy, like inside a hollow stump.

In winter snow piles up to the roof, and sometimes we have to dig our way to the door. In spring wild Johnny-jump-ups bloom by the porch, and in summer all the nearby bushes are loaded with huckleberries. In fall the vine maple leaves turn bright autumn colors. The yellow ones look like sunshine in the woods, even on rainy days.

It's a little dark in here, but when Mom pulls back the curtains, the light will be just right. It's a little cold, too, because it's winter, but as soon as Dad gets the wood stove going and logs burning in the fireplace, we'll all be toasty warm.

Dad says our cabin is too full of everything, but it's all stuff we want to keep forever. The ox yoke, hanging above the fireplace, is from pioneer days. My great-grandfather found it on an abandoned farm. The snowshoes were worn by my great-great-uncle when he went fur trapping in the Yukon. My grandfather painted all the paintings during a war, when he was out in the South Pacific ocean. The Navajo rug, the tápa cloth, and all the toys have always been here.

The cabin got electricity when Mom was about my age, but we don't use it much. We'd rather burn kerosene lamps like they did in the olden days. We use a carpet sweeper instead of a vacuum cleaner and keep food cold in an icebox instead of in a refrigerator. We don't have a bathroom inside, but that's OK. We have an outhouse around in back.

We don't have running water, either. Dad says we do, though—when I run down to the creek and run back with buckets full! Mom fills basins for us to wash up in, and if we get really dirty, she heats water on top of the wood stove and fills a big tub for our baths.

Bringing in water is one of the first things I do when we get to the cabin. I have to be careful, because if I hurry too fast down the creek bank, especially in the snow, I'll slip and slide right into the water.

In summer I like to go fishing in this creek. Dad says the fish are here all year, but I didn't see any today, not even one.

Sometimes I see animal tracks in the snow. Cougars live around here, but I've only seen their footprints. Deer and elk aren't here now. They've moved down to where the weather is warmer and food is easier to find. Bears are hibernating for the winter, but they'll be back after the snow melts.

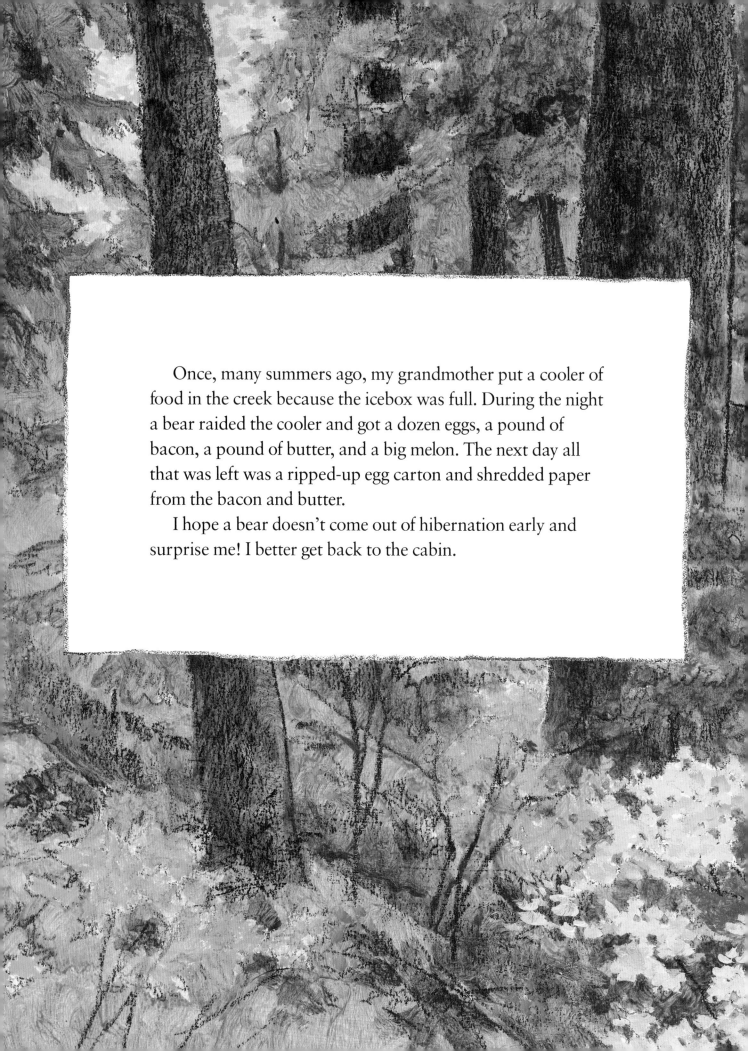

Once, many summers ago, my grandmother put a cooler of food in the creek because the icebox was full. During the night a bear raided the cooler and got a dozen eggs, a pound of bacon, a pound of butter, and a big melon. The next day all that was left was a ripped-up egg carton and shredded paper from the bacon and butter.

I hope a bear doesn't come out of hibernation early and surprise me! I better get back to the cabin.

This tree, right here by our porch, is my favorite. Years ago Mom and my uncle used to climb it. Both of them were little then, and the tree was little, too. They would go clear to the top and swing the whole tree back and forth. Now the tree is too tall for me to get near the top, and too strong for me to swing it at all. Maybe someday I can get my uncle to climb up there with me, and we could swing the tree back and forth together.

Those two whistling birds, high in the tree, are nervy "camp robbers." If I had some bread with me, they'd eat it out of my hands—or off the top of my head. I love to feed camp robbers.

I'd love to feed an elk, too. Once, a long time ago, my uncle was at the cabin all alone. In the middle of the night he heard heavy footsteps on the porch. When he opened the door he was face to face with a big cow elk. Elk never come that close to people, so my uncle knew something must be wrong. He thought the elk might be starving. He fed her fresh vegetables, and she ate them all.

Better get this water inside before it starts to freeze in the buckets. Maybe Mom will heat some and make me a big mug of hot chocolate.

Then, before it gets too dark,
Dad needs me to help him fill the
woodshed. He chops the wood,
and I stack it.

Mom wants me to look through our trunkful of decorations. We're coming back to the cabin for Christmas, and we have to be sure that the mice haven't gotten into the trunk and chewed up our old-fashioned ribbon-covered ornaments. We always hang these ornaments on the tree we put up in the cabin's front window. In the trunk we have bunting and flags we fly off the porch on the Fourth of July, too, and fold-out paper turkeys and pumpkins we put on our Thanksgiving table.

Mom says that the best decoration the cabin ever had was years ago, when there was a big snowfall on Christmas Eve. My grandfather built an igloo on the front porch and put lots of lighted candles inside. It looked like the biggest, most beautiful Christmas ornament ever.

Dad fries steaks in a big heavy skillet, right on the coals in the fireplace, for our dinner. I love to hear the steaks sizzle in that real hot pan. While Mom heats canned spuds on the stove, I set the table with my great-grandmother's enameled tin dishes. Dad doesn't like the sound forks make on the metal plates, and Mom says the cup handles get too hot to hold, but I really like these dishes. They're old, ten times older than I am.

After dinner we wind up our phonograph and play ancient records. A phonograph makes very good, scratchy-sounding music. Dad reads to me, too. There are the best stories in those books up on the little library shelf above the sofa.

When it's time to get ready for
bed, I put on my warmest pajamas,
my robe, and my snow boots. Then,
like I always do, I go out onto the
porch, brush my teeth, and spit over
the porch railing into the snow.

Brrr, it's cold out there. Feels good to get back inside.

After I pick out which heavy quilt I want to sleep under, Mom and I make up my bed. I sleep by the window that looks toward the creek.

As soon as all the lights are out and I'm snuggled in my bed, Mom tells scary stories.

Sometimes they're about the mice that live in our cabin, but those stories don't scare me too much. I'm used to mice. At night we hear them playing and scampering around for crumbs, running all over the place. If we forget to put cups over the spouts, they even get inside the big teakettle or the old camp coffeepot and run around in there.

Mom's telling a ghost story tonight, all about a ghost that is flying around in our rafters. I think I just saw it fly through those creepy shadows the dying fire is making on the ceiling. If I pull the quilt over my head and plug my ears with my fingers, I won't see or hear anything scary at all.

I'll just cuddle down in my warm bed
and think about when I'm old like Mom
and Dad. I'll bring my own kids here.
They'll get water from the creek, feed the
camp robbers, stack wood, set the table
with the tin dishes, and listen to stories.
When they're big enough, they'll even
unlock the cabin door with my cabin key.

To Ted's mother, Martha, who found this
mountain place and brought it into our family.

Special thanks to Diane D'Andrade, who
heard a book in our stories about our cabin.
—G. R. and T. R.

Text copyright © 1994 by Gloria Rand
Illustrations copyright © 1994 by Ted Rand

Requests for permission to make copies of any part of the work should
be mailed to:
Permissions Department, Harcourt Brace & Company, Publishers,
6277 Sea Harbor Drive, Orlando, Florida 32887-6777.

Library of Congress Cataloging-in-Publication Data
Rand, Gloria.
The cabin key/by Gloria Rand; illustrated by Ted Rand.—1st ed.
p. cm.
Summary: Reveling in the atmosphere of her family's mountain cabin,
a young girl remembers the many stories she has heard about previous
generations and their adventures with the area's wildlife.
ISBN 0-15-213884-6
[1. Nature—Fiction. 2. Family life—Fiction.] I. Rand, Ted. ill. II. Title.
PZ7.R1553Cab 1994
[E]—dc20   93-10398

First edition
A B C D E

The illustrations in this book were drawn in jumbo wax crayon
and painted in acrylics on gesso-coated 100 percent rag stock.
The display type was set in Pabst by Harcourt Brace & Company
Photocomposition Center, San Diego, California.
The text type was set in Sabon by Central Graphics, San Diego,
California.
Color separations were made by Bright Arts, Ltd., Singapore.
Printed and bound by Tien Wah Press, Singapore
Production supervision by Warren Wallerstein and Cheryl Kennedy
Designed by Lydia D'moch